PENGUIN BOOKS

Paris for One

Jojo Moyes is a novelist and a journalist. She
worked at the *Independent* for ten years before
leaving to write full-time. Her previous novels
have all been critically acclaimed and include
The Girl You Left Behind, *Me Before You* and
The One Plus One. She lives in Essex with her
husband and their three children.

Paris for One

Jojo Moyes

PENGUIN BOOKS

PENGUIN BOOKS

UK | USA | Canada | Ireland | Australia
India | New Zealand | South Africa

Penguin Books is part of the Penguin Random House
group of companies whose addresses can be found at
global.penguinrandomhouse.com.

First published 2014
001

Copyright © Jojo Moyes, 2014

The moral right of the author has been asserted

Set in 12/16 pt Stone Serif
Typeset by Palimpsest Book Production Limited, Falkirk, Stirlingshire
Printed in Great Britain by Clays Ltd, St Ives plc

A CIP catalogue record for this book is available from
the British Library

ISBN: 978–1–405–91893–0

www.greenpenguin.co.uk

Penguin Random House is committed to a
sustainable future for our business, our readers
and our planet. This book is made from Forest
Stewardship Council® certified paper.

Paris for One

Chapter One

Nell shifts her bag along the plastic seating in the station and checks the clock on the wall for the eighty-ninth time. Her gaze flicks back as the door from Security slides open. Another family – Disney-bound – walks through into the departure lounge, with buggy, screaming children and parents who have been awake way too long.

For the last half-hour her heart has been thumping, a sick feeling high in her chest.

'He will come. He will still come. He can still make it,' she says under her breath.

'Train 9051 to Paris will be leaving from platform two in ten minutes. Please make your way to the platform. Remember to take all luggage with you.'

She chews her lip, then texts him again – the fifth time.

Where are you? Train about to leave!

She had texted him twice as she set off, checking that they were still meeting at the station. When he didn't answer, she told herself it was because she had been on the Underground. Or he had. She sends a third text, and a fourth. And then, as she stands there, her phone vibrates in her hand.

Sorry babe. Caught up at work. Not going to make it.

As if they had planned to catch up over a quick drink after work. She stares at the phone in disbelief.

Not going to make this train? Shall I wait?

And, seconds later, the reply:

No, you go. Will try to get later train.

She is too shocked to be angry. She stands still, as people get to their feet around her, pulling on coats, and punches out a reply.

But where will we meet?

2

He doesn't answer. *Caught up at work.* It's a surf- and scuba-wear shop. In November. How caught up can he be?

She gazes around her, as if this might still be a joke. As if he will, even now, burst through the doors, with his wide smile, telling her that he was teasing her (he is a bit too fond of teasing her). And he will take her arm, kiss her cheek with wind-chilled lips, and say something like 'You didn't think I'd miss this, did you? Your first trip to Paris?'

But the glass doors stay firmly shut.

'Madam? You need to go to the platform.' The Eurostar guard reaches for her ticket. And for a second she hesitates – *will he come?* – and then she is in the crowd, her little case trailing behind her. She stops and types:

Meet me at the hotel then.

She heads down the escalator as the huge train roars into the station.

'What do you mean, you're not coming? We've planned this for ages.' It is the annual Girls' Trip to Brighton. They have gone there on the first weekend of November, every year for six years – Nell, Magda, Trish and Sue – piled into Sue's old four-wheel drive or Magda's company car. They would escape their daily lives for two nights of drinking, hanging out with the lads from stag weekends and nursing hangovers over cooked breakfasts in a tatty hotel called Brightsea Lodge.

The annual trip has survived through two babies, one divorce, and a case of shingles (they spent the first night partying in Magda's hotel room instead). Nobody has ever missed one.

'Well, Pete's invited me to go to Paris.'

'Pete is taking you to Paris?' Magda had stared at her, as if she'd announced she was learning to speak Russian. '*Pete* Pete?'

'He says he can't believe I've never been.'

'I went to Paris once, on a school trip. I got lost in the Louvre and someone put my trainer down a toilet in the youth hostel,' said Trish.

'I snogged a French boy because he looked like that bloke who goes out with Hallé Berry.'

'*Pete-with-the-hair* Pete? *Your* Pete? I don't mean to sound mean. I just thought he was a bit of a . . .'

'Loser,' said Sue, helpfully.

'Knob.'

'Prat.'

'Obviously we're wrong. Turns out he's the

kind of bloke who takes Nell on dirty weekends to Paris. Which is . . . you know. Great. I just wish it wasn't the same weekend as *our* weekend.'

'Well, once we'd got the tickets . . . it was difficult . . .' Nell mumbled, with a wave of her hand, hoping nobody would ask who had got these tickets. (It had been the only weekend left before Christmas when the discount had applied.)

She had planned the trip as carefully as she organized her office paperwork. She had searched the internet for the best places to go, scanning TripAdvisor for the best budget hotels, cross-checking each one on Google, and entering the results on a spreadsheet.

She had settled on a place behind the Rue de Rivoli – 'clean, friendly, very romantic' – and booked it for two nights. She pictured herself and Pete, tangled up in a French hotel bed, gazing out of the window at the Eiffel Tower, holding hands over croissants and coffee in some street café. She was only really going on pictures: she didn't have much idea what you did on a weekend in Paris, apart from the obvious.

At the age of twenty-six, Nell Simmons had never been away for a weekend with a boyfriend, unless you counted that time she went rock-climbing with Andrew Dinsmore. He had made them sleep in his Mini and she woke up so cold that she couldn't move her neck for six hours.

Nell's mother was fond of telling anyone who would listen that Nell 'was not the adventurous type'. She was also 'not the type to travel', 'not the kind of girl who can rely on her looks', and now, finally, 'no spring chicken'.

That was the thing about growing up in a small town – everyone thought they knew what you were. Nell was the sensible one. The quiet one. The one who would carefully research any plan and who could be trusted to water your plants, mind your kids, and not run off with anyone's husband.

No, Mother. What I really am, Nell thought, as she printed off the tickets, gazing at them, then tucking them into a folder with all the important information, is the kind of girl who goes to Paris for the weekend.

As the big day grew nearer, she started to enjoy dropping it into conversation. 'Got to make sure my passport is up–to-date,' she said, when she left her mother after Sunday lunch. She bought new underwear, shaved her legs, painted her toenails a vivid shade of red (she usually went for clear). 'Don't forget I'm leaving early on Friday,' she said at work. 'For Paris.'

'Oh, you're so lucky,' chorused the girls in Accounts.

'I'm well jell,' said Trish, who disliked Pete slightly less than everyone else.

Nell climbs onto the train and stows her bag, wondering how 'jell' Trish would be if she could see her now: a girl beside an empty seat going to Paris with no idea if her boyfriend was going to turn up.

Chapter Two

The train station in Paris is busy. She emerges through the platform gates and is frozen to the spot, standing in the middle of the crowd of people, all pushing and shoving. She feels lost among the glass kiosks and escalators that seem to lead nowhere.

A three-note chime sounds on the loud-speaker and the station announcer says something in French that Nell can't understand. Everyone else is walking briskly, as if they know where they're going. It is dark outside and she fights panic. *I'm in a strange city and I don't even speak the language.* And then she sees the sign: Taxis.

The queue is fifty people long, but she doesn't care. She scrabbles in her bag for the hotel print-out, and when she finally reaches the front of the queue, she holds it out. 'Hôtel Bonne Ville,' she says. 'Um . . . *s'il vous plaît.*'

The driver looks back at her, as if he cannot understand what she says.

'Hôtel Bonne Ville,' she says, trying to sound French. 'Bonne Ville.'

He looks blank and snatches the piece of paper from her. He stares at it for a moment.

'Ah! Hôtel Bonne Ville!' he says, lifting his eyes to heaven. He thrusts the piece of paper back at her, and pulls out into the heavy traffic.

Nell sits back in the seat and lets out a long breath.

And welcome to Paris.

The journey takes twenty long, expensive minutes. The traffic is terrible. She gazes out of the window at the busy streets, the hairdressers and nail bars, repeating the French road signs under her breath. The elegant grey buildings rise high into the city sky, and the coffee shops glow in the winter night. Paris, she thinks, and feels suddenly that it will be OK. Pete will come later. She will be waiting for him at the hotel, and tomorrow they will laugh at how worried she was about travelling alone. He always said she was too much of a worrier.

Chill out, babe, he will say. Pete never got stressed about anything. He'd travelled the world. When he had got held up at gunpoint in Laos, he said, he had just chilled. 'No point getting stressed. They were either going to shoot me or they weren't. Nothing I could do about it.' Then he nodded. 'We ended up going for a beer with those soldiers.'

Or there was the time when he was on a small ferry in Kenya, which overturned. 'We just cut the tyres off the sides of the boat and hung on till help came. I was pretty relaxed about that too – till they told me there were crocodiles in the water.'

She sometimes wondered why Pete, with his tanned features and his endless life experiences, had chosen her. She wasn't flashy or wild. He once told her he liked her because she didn't give him a hard time. 'Other girlfriends are like this in my ear.' He mimed a nipping motion with his hands. 'You're . . . relaxing to be with.'

Sometimes Nell wondered if this made her sound a bit like a DFS sofa, but it was probably best not to question these things too hard.

Paris.

She winds down the window, taking in the sounds of the busy streets, the scent of perfume, coffee and smoke. It is just as she'd pictured it. The buildings are tall, with long windows and little balconies – there are no office blocks. Every street corner seems to have a café, with round tables and chairs outside. And as the taxi heads further into the city, the women look

10

more stylish, and people are greeting each other with kisses as they stop on the pavement.

I'm actually in Paris, she thinks. And suddenly she is grateful that she has a couple of hours to freshen up before Pete arrives. For once she does not want to be the wide-eyed innocent.

I'm going to be Parisian, she thinks, and sinks back in her seat.

The hotel is in a narrow street off a main road. She counts out the euros according to the sum on the taxi's meter, but instead of taking it, the driver acts as if she has insulted him, waving towards her suitcase in the boot.

'I'm sorry. I don't understand,' she says. Then, after a pause, she anxiously gives him another ten euros. He takes the money, shakes his head, then puts her suitcase on the pavement. She stands there as he drives off and wonders if she has just been ripped off.

But the hotel looks nice. She will not let anything upset her. She walks in, and finds herself in a narrow lobby. Already she's wondering what Pete will think of it. 'Not bad,' he will say, nodding. *Not bad, babe.*

'Hello,' she says, nervous, and then, because she has no idea how to say it in French, 'I have booked a room.'

11

Another woman has arrived behind her, huffing and puffing as she scrabbles in her bag for her own paperwork.

'Yeah. I have a room booked too.' She slaps her own paperwork on the desk beside Nell's. Nell shifts to the side, and tries not to feel crowded.

'Ugh. I have had a *nightmare* getting here. *A nightmare.*' The woman is American. 'The traffic is the *pits*.'

The receptionist is in her forties, with short well-cut black hair. She glances up at the two women with a frown. 'You both have bookings?'

She leans forward and examines the bits of paper. Then she pushes each one towards its owner. 'But I have only one room left. We are fully booked.'

'That's impossible. You confirmed the booking.' The American woman pushes the paper back at her. 'I booked it last week.'

'Me too,' says Nell. 'I booked mine two weeks ago. Look, you can see on my bit of paper.'

The two women stare at each other, suddenly aware that they are in competition.

'I am sorry. I do not know how you have this booking. We only have one room.' The Frenchwoman makes it sound as if it is their fault.

'Well, you will have to find us another room. You must honour the bookings. Look, there they are in black and white. I know my rights.'

The Frenchwoman lifts a perfectly plucked eyebrow. 'Madame. I cannot give you what I do not have. There is one room, with a twin bed or a double bed, depending on how you want us to arrange it. I can offer one of you a refund, but I do not have two rooms.'

'But I can't go anywhere else. I'm meant to be meeting someone,' says Nell. 'He won't know where I am.'

'I'm not moving,' says the American, folding her arms. 'I have just flown six thousand miles and I have a dinner to go to. I have no time to find somewhere else.'

'Then you may share the room. I can offer each of you a discount of fifty per cent and I will ask the maid to turn the bed into two singles.'

'Share a room with a stranger? You have got to be kidding me,' says the American.

'Then I suggest you find another hotel,' says the receptionist coolly, and turns to answer a telephone.

Nell and the American woman stare at each other. The American woman says, 'I have just got off a flight from Chicago.'

13

Nell says, 'I've never been to Paris before. I don't know where I would find another hotel.'

Neither of them moves. Nell says finally, 'Look – my boyfriend is meant to be meeting me here. We could both take our cases up for now, and when he arrives I'll see if he can find us another hotel. He knows Paris better than I do.'

The American woman looks her up and down slowly, as if working out whether to trust her. 'I'm not sharing with two of you.'

Nell holds her gaze. 'Believe me, that is not my idea of a fun weekend away either.'

'I don't suppose we have a lot of choice,' the woman says. 'I can't believe this is happening.'

They inform the receptionist of their plan. The American woman says, 'And when this lady leaves I still want my fifty per cent discount. This whole thing is shameful. You would never get away with service like this where I come from.'

Nell wonders if she has ever been more uncomfortable, trapped between the French-woman's lack of interest and the American's resentment. She tries to imagine what Pete would do. He would laugh, take it all in his stride. His ability to laugh at life is one of the things she finds attractive about him. It's fine, she tells herself. They will joke about it later.

They take the key and share a tiny lift up to the third floor. Nell walks behind. The door opens onto an attic room with two beds.

'Oh,' says the American. 'No bath. I hate that there's no bath. And it's so *small.*'

Nell drops her bag and texts Pete to tell him, and asks if he can find another hotel.

I'll wait here for you. Can you let me know whether you'll arrive in time for supper? Am quite hungry.

It is already eight o'clock.

He doesn't respond. She wonders if he is in the Channel tunnel: if he is, he is at least an hour and a half away. She sits in silence as the American woman huffs and puffs and opens her suitcase on the bed, taking all the hangers as she hangs up her clothes.

'Are you here on business?' says Nell, when the silence becomes too heavy.

'Two meetings. One tonight, and then a day off. I haven't had a day off this month.' The American says this as if it is Nell's fault. 'And tomorrow I have to be on the other side of Paris. Right. I've got to go out now. I'm going to trust that you won't touch my stuff.'

Nell stares at her. 'I'm not going to touch your stuff.'

'I don't mean to be rude. It's just I'm not in the habit of sharing rooms with total strangers. When your boyfriend arrives, I'd be glad if you could hand in your key downstairs.'

Nell tries not to show her anger. 'I'll do that,' she says, and picks up her book, pretending to read as, with a backward glance, the American leaves the room. And it is just at this moment that her phone beeps. Nell snatches it up.

Sorry babe. Not going to get there. Have a great trip.

Chapter Three

Fabien sits on the rooftop, pulls his woollen hat further down over his eyes and lights another cigarette. It is the spot he always used to smoke when there was a chance that Sandrine would come back. She hadn't liked the smell, and if he smoked inside she used to screw up her nose and say that the studio apartment smelt disgusting.

It is a narrow ledge, but big enough for a tall man and a mug of coffee and 332 pages of handwritten manuscript. In summer he sometimes naps out here, and waves to the teenage twins across the square. They sit on their own flat roof to listen to music and smoke, away from the gaze of their parents.

Central Paris is full of such spaces. If you don't have a garden, or a tiny balcony, you find your outside space where you can.

Fabien picks up his pencil and starts crossing out words. He has been editing this manuscript for six months and now the lines of writing are thick with pencil marks. Every time he reads his novel he sees more faults.

The characters are flat, their voices fake. Philippe, his friend, says he has to get a move on, get it typed and give it to the agent who is interested. But every time he looks at it, he sees more reasons why he cannot show anyone his book.

It is not ready.

Sandrine said he didn't want to hand it over because, until he did, he could still tell himself he had hope. It was one of the less cruel things she had said.

He checks his watch, knowing he has only an hour before he has to start his shift. And then he hears his mobile phone ringing. Damn! It is inside. He curses himself for forgetting to tuck it into his pocket before coming out on to the roof. He balances his mug on the pile of pages, to stop them blowing away, and turns to climb back in through the window.

Afterwards, he is not sure quite what happened. His right foot slips on the desk that he uses to climb back in and his left foot shoots backwards as he tries to stop himself falling. And his foot – his great clumsy foot, as Sandrine would call it – kicks the mug and the pages off the ledge. He turns in time to hear the mug smash on the cobbles below, and to watch 332 white pages fly out into the darkening skies.

He watches his pages catch the wind and, like white doves, float into the streets of Paris.

Chapter Four

Nell has spent an hour lying on the bed and she still cannot work out what to do. Pete is not coming to Paris. He is actually not coming. She has come all the way to the capital of France, with new underwear and painted red toenails, and Pete has stood her up.

For the first ten minutes she had stared at the message – its cheery 'have a great trip' – and waited for more. But, no, he really was not coming.

She lies on the bed, her phone still in her hand, staring at the wall. She realizes some part of her had always known this might happen. She peers at the phone, flicks the screen on and off, just to make sure she is not dreaming.

But she knows. She probably knew it last night, when he didn't respond to her calls. She might even have known it last week when all her ideas for what they might do in Paris were met with 'Yeah, whatever', or 'I don't know'.

It was not just that Pete was an unreliable

boyfriend – in fact, he often disappeared without telling her where he was going. If she was honest with herself, he hadn't actually invited her.

They had been talking about places they had been and she had admitted that she had never been to Paris, and he'd said, vaguely, 'Really? Oh, it's awesome. You'd love it.'

It was the only truly impulsive thing she'd ever done in her life. Two nights later, she had been looking at the website and seen the Eurostar special offer. Her finger had hovered over the *book* button on her computer and, before she knew what she was doing, she had bought two return tickets. She had presented him with them, glowing half with embarrassment, half with pleasure, the next night when they had gone back to his place.

'You did what?' He had been drunk, she remembered now, and he had blinked slowly, as if in disbelief. 'You bought me a ticket to Paris?'

'Us,' she had said, as he fumbled with the buttons of her dress. 'A weekend in Paris. I thought it would be . . . fun.'

'You bought me a ticket to Paris!' He had shaken his head, his hair flopping over one eye. And then he said, 'Sure, babe. Why not?

21

Nice one.' She couldn't remember what else he'd said, as they'd collapsed onto his bed.

Now she will have to go back to the station, and back to England and tell Magda, Trish and Sue that they were right. That Pete was exactly who they said he was. That she had been a fool and wasted her money. She had blown out the Girls' Trip to Brighton for nothing.

She screws her eyes shut, until she is sure that she will not cry, then pushes herself upright. She looks at her suitcase. She wonders where to find a taxi, and whether her ticket can be changed. What if she gets to the station and they will not let her on the train? She wonders whether to ask the receptionist down-stairs if she will ring Eurostar for her, but she is afraid of the woman's icy gaze. She has no idea what to do.

Her phone beeps again. She snatches it up, her heart suddenly racing. He is coming after all! It will be all right! But it is Magda.

Having fun, you filthy mare?

She blinks at it, and suddenly feels horribly homesick. She wishes she was there, in Magda's hotel room, a plastic cup of cheap fizz on the bathroom sink as they fight for mirror space to put on their make-up. England is an hour behind. They will still be getting ready, their suitcases spilling new outfits onto the carpet, the music turned up loud enough to cause complaints.

She thinks, briefly, that she has never felt so lonely in her life.

All great, thanks. Have fun!

She types slowly and presses SEND, waiting for the whooshing sound that tells her it has flown across the English Channel. And then she turns off her phone so that she will not have to lie any more.

Nell examines the Eurostar timetable, pulls her notebook from her bag and writes a list, working out her options. It is a quarter to nine. Even if she makes it back to the station, she is unlikely to get a train that will take her back to England early enough for her to get home. She will have to stay here tonight.

In the harsh light of the bathroom mirror, she looks tired and fed up. She looks exactly like the kind of girl who has just travelled all the way to Paris to be stood up by her boyfriend. She rests her hands on the sink, takes a long, shaky breath, and tries to think clearly.

She will find something to eat, get some sleep, and then she will feel better. Tomorrow she will catch the early train home. It is not what she had hoped, but it is a plan, and Nell always feels better with a plan.

She shuts the door, locks it and goes downstairs. She tries to look carefree and confident, like a woman who often finds herself alone in strange cities.

'Do you know anywhere nice I could get a bite to eat?' she asks the receptionist.

The woman looks at her. 'You want a restaurant?'

'Or café. Anything. Somewhere I could walk to. Oh, and – um – if the other lady comes back, will you tell her I'll be staying this evening?'

The Frenchwoman raises an eyebrow a fraction, and Nell imagines her thinking: So your boyfriend never turned up, mousy English girl? That's no surprise. 'There is Café des Bastides,' she says, handing over a small tourist map. 'You turn right outside, and it's two streets down on the left. It's very nice. Fine to . . .' she pauses '. . . eat alone.'

'Thank you.' Nell, her cheeks flaming, grabs the map, slides it into her handbag, and walks briskly from the hotel lobby.

*

The café is busy, but Nell finds a small table and chair in a corner by the window and slides in. There is a steamy fug on the inside of the windows, and around her people chat in French. She feels self-conscious, as if she is wearing a sign that says, PITY ME. I HAVE NOBODY TO EAT WITH. She gazes up at the blackboard, saying the words in her head several times before she has to speak them aloud.

'*Bonsoir.*' The waiter, who has a shaven head and a long white apron, puts a jug of water in front of her. '*Qu'est-ce –*'

'*Je voudrais le steak frites s'il vous plaît,*' she says in a rush. Her meal – steak and chips – is expensive, but it is the only thing she thinks she can pronounce without sounding silly.

The waiter gives a small nod and glances behind him, as if distracted. 'The steak? And to drink, Mam'selle?' he says, in perfect English. 'Some wine?'

She was going to have Coke. But she whispers, 'Yes, please.'

'*Bon,*' he says. In minutes he is back with a basket of bread and a jug of wine. He puts them down as if it is normal for a woman to be sitting there on a Friday evening by herself, and then he is gone.

25

Nell doesn't think she has ever seen a woman sitting alone in a restaurant, apart from that time when she went on a sales trip to Corby and that woman sat alone with her book by the Ladies and ate two desserts instead of a main course. Where she lives, girls eat out in groups, mostly curry at the end of a long night's drinking. Older women might go alone to bingo, or to a family event. But women don't just go out and eat alone.

But, as she looks around her now and chews a piece of crusty French bread, she sees that she is not the only single diner. There is a woman on the other side of the window, a jug of red wine on her table, smoking a cigarette as she watches the people of Paris bustle by. There is a man in the corner reading his paper, spooning forkfuls of something into his mouth. Another woman, long hair, a gap in her teeth, is chatting to a waiter, her collar high around her neck. Nobody is paying them any attention. Nell relaxes a little, unwinding her scarf.

The wine is good. She takes a sip and feels the tension of the day start to ooze away. She has another sip. The steak arrives, seared brown and steaming, but when she cuts into it, it is bloody inside. She wonders whether to send it back, but she doesn't want to make a fuss, especially not in French.

Besides, it tastes good. The chips are crisp and golden and hot, and the green salad is delicious. She eats it all, surprising herself with her appetite. The waiter, when he returns, smiles at her evident pleasure. 'Is good, uh?'

'Delicious,' she says. 'Thank – er, *merci*.' He nods, and refills her glass. As she reaches for it, she manages to knock half of the red wine onto the waiter's apron and shoes, leaving deep red stains.

'I'm so sorry!' Her hands fly to her mouth.

He sighs wearily, as he mops at himself. 'Really. It's of no matter.'

'I'm sorry. Oh, I –'

'Really. No matter.'

He gives her a vague smile, and disappears.

She feels her cheeks burning red and pulls her notebook from her bag, to give herself something to do. She flicks quickly past her list for sightseeing in Paris, and stares at an empty page until she is sure nobody is looking.

Live in the moment, she writes on the clean page, and underlines it twice. It is something she once saw in a magazine. *And maybe don't spill stuff.*

She looks up at the clock. It is nine forty-five.

Only about 39,600 more moments, and then she can get back on the train and pretend this trip never happened.

The Frenchwoman is still behind the reception desk when Nell returns to the hotel. Of course she is. She slides the key across the counter towards Nell. 'The other lady is not back yet,' the woman says. She pronounces it *ze uzzer*. 'If she returns before I finish I will let her know you are in the room.'

Nell mutters a thank-you and heads upstairs.

She runs a shower and steps under it, trying to wash away the disappointment of the day. Finally, at half past ten, she climbs into bed and reads one of the French magazines from the bedside table. She doesn't understand most of the words, but she hasn't brought a book. She hadn't expected to spend any time reading.

Finally, at eleven, she turns off the light and lies in the dark, listening to the sound of mopeds whizzing down the narrow streets, and to the chatter of happy French people making their way home. She feels as if she has been locked out of a giant party.

Her eyes fill with tears, and she wonders whether to call the girls and tell them what has happened. But she is not ready for their sympathy. She does not let herself think about Pete, and that she has been dumped. She tries not to imagine her mother's face when she has to tell her the truth about her romantic weekend away.

And then the door opens. The light flicks on.

'I don't believe it.' The American woman stands there, her face flushed with drink, a large purple scarf draped around her shoulders.

'I thought you would be gone.'

'So did I,' said Nell, pulling the covers over her head. 'Would you mind turning down the light please?'

'They never said you were still here.'

'Well, I am.'

She hears the clunk of a handbag on the table, the rattle of hangers in the wardrobe. 'I do not feel comfortable spending the night with somebody I don't know in the room.'

'Believe me, you were not my first choice for tonight's sleeping companion either.'

Nell stays under the covers while the woman fusses about and goes in and out of the bathroom. She hears her scrubbing her teeth, gargling, the flush of a loo through walls that are far too thin. She tries to imagine she is somewhere else. In Brighton, maybe, with one of the girls, drunkenly making her way to bed.

'I might as well tell you, I am not happy,' the woman says.

'Well, sleep somewhere else,' snaps Nell. 'Because I have just as much right to this room as you. More, if you think about the dates on our bookings.'

'There's no need to be snappy,' said the woman.

'Well, there's no need to make me feel worse than I already bloody do.'

'Honey, it's not my fault your boyfriend didn't turn up.'

'And it's not *my* fault the hotel double booked us.'

There is a long silence. Nell wonders, briefly, if the woman is about to say something friendly. It is daft, after all, two women fighting in such a small space. We are in the same boat, she thinks. She tries to think of something friendly to say.

And then the woman's voice cuts across the dark: 'Well, just so as you know, I'm putting my valuables in the safe. And I am trained in self-defence.'

'And my name is Queen Elizabeth the Second,' Nell mutters. She raises her eyes to heaven in the dark, and waits for the click that tells her the light has gone out.

*

Even though she is exhausted and a bit sad, Nell can't get to sleep. She tries to relax, to calm her thoughts, but around midnight, a voice in her mind says: *Nope. No sleep for you, lady.*

Instead, her brain spins and churns like a washing machine, throwing up black thoughts like so much dirty laundry. Had she been too keen? Was she not cool enough? Was it because of her list of French art galleries, with their pros and cons (length of journey time versus possible queue)?

Was she just too boring for any man to love?

The night stretches and sags. She lies in the dark, trying to block her ears against the sound of the stranger snoring in the next bed. She tries stretching, yawning, changing her position. She tries deep breathing, relaxing bits of her body, and imagining her darker thoughts locked in a box and herself throwing away the key.

At around three in the morning, she accepts she will probably be awake until dawn. She gets up and pads over to the window, pulling the curtain a few inches away from the glass.

The rooftops glow under the street-lamps. A light drizzle falls silently onto the pavement. A couple, their heads close, make their way slowly home, murmuring to each other.

This should have been so wonderful, she thinks.

The American woman's snoring is louder. She snorts, sounding like someone choking. Nell reaches into her suitcase for ear plugs (she had brought two pairs, just in case) and climbs back into bed. I will be home in a little over eight hours, she thinks, and with that comforting thought, she finally drifts off to sleep.

Chapter Five

At the café, Fabien sits by the kitchen hatch, watching as Emil scrubs at the huge steel pans. He is sipping a large coffee, and his shoulders slump. The clock says a quarter to one.

'You'll write another one. It will be better,' says Emil.

'I put everything I had into that book. And now it's all gone.'

'Come on. You say you are a writer. You must have more than one book in your head. If not, you will be a very hungry writer. And maybe next time, do it on a computer, yes? Then you can just print out another copy.'

Fabien had found 183 pages of the 300-plus that had blown away. Some of them were blurred with dirt and rain-water, stamped with footprints. Others had disappeared into the Paris evening. As he walked the streets around his home he had seen the odd page, flying into the air, or sodden in a gutter, ignored by passers-by. Seeing his words out there, his innermost thoughts, made him feel as if he were standing in the street stark naked.

'I'm such a fool, Emil. Sandrine told me so many times not to take my work out on the roof . . .'

'Oh, no. Not a Sandrine story. Please!' Emil empties the sink of greasy water and refills it. 'I need some brandy if we are going to have a Sandrine story.'

'What am I going to do?'

'What your great hero, the writer Samuel Beckett, tells you to do: "Try again. Fail again. Fail better."'

Emil looks up, his brown skin glistening with sweat and steam. 'And I'm not just talking about the book. You need to get out there again. Meet some women. Drink a little, dance a little . . . Find some material for another book!'

'I don't know. I'm not really in the mood.'

'Then put yourself in the mood!' Emil is like a radiator, always making you feel warmer. 'At least you have a reason to get out of that apartment now, uh? Go and live a little. Think about something else.'

He finishes the last pan. He stacks it with the others, then flicks the tea-towel over his shoulder.

'Okay. Olivier is working his shift tomorrow

night, yes? So you and me. Out for some beers. What do you say?'

'I don't know . . .'

'Well, what else are you going to do? Spend the night in your tiny apartment. Monsieur Hollande, our president, on the television will tell you there is no money. Your empty home will tell you there is no woman.'

'You're not making things sound any better, Emil.'

'I am! I am your friend! I am giving you a million reasons to come out with me. Come on, we'll have some laughs. Pick up some bad women. Get arrested.'

Fabien finishes his coffee and hands the cup to Emil, who puts it in the sink.

'Come on. You have to live so that you have something to write about.'

'Maybe,' he says. 'I'll think about it.'

Chapter Six

It is the knocking that wakes her. It comes to her at first from a distance, getting louder, then she hears a voice: 'Housekeeping.'

Housekeeping.

Nell pushes herself upright, blinking, a faint ringing in her ears, and for a moment she has no idea where she is. She stares at the strange bed, then at the wallpaper. There is a muffled rapping sound. She reaches up to her ears, and pulls out the plugs. Suddenly the sound is deafening.

She walks over to the door and opens it, rubbing her eyes. 'Hello?'

The woman – in a maid's uniform – apologises, steps back and says something in what must be French.

But Nell has no idea what. So she nods and lets the door close. She feels like she has been run over. She glances at the American woman, but there is only an empty bed, the cover ruffled and the wardrobe door hanging open. She glances over, panicky, at her suitcase, but it is still there.

She hadn't realised the woman was going to leave so early, but Nell is relieved not to have to face that cross red face again. Now she can shower in peace and –

She glances down at her phone. It is a quarter past eleven.

It can't be.

She flicks on the television, skipping through until she hits a news channel.

It really is a quarter past eleven.

Suddenly awake, she begins to gather up her things, dumping them in her suitcase, and pulls on her clothes. Then, grabbing the key and her tickets, she runs downstairs. The Frenchwoman is behind the desk, as perfect as she had been last night. Nell wishes suddenly that she had paused to brush her hair.

'Good morning, Mademoiselle.'

'Good morning. I wondered if you could . . . if . . . Well, I need to change my Eurostar ticket.'

'You would like me to call Eurostar?'

'Please. I need to get home today. A . . . family emergency.'

The woman's face does not flicker. 'Of course.'

She takes the ticket and dials, and then speaks

in rapid French. Nell runs her fingers through her hair, then rubs sleep from her eyes.

'They have nothing until five o'clock. Will this suit you?'

'Nothing at all?'

'There were some spaces on the early trains this morning, but nothing now until five.'

Nell curses herself for sleeping late. 'That's fine.'

'And you will have to buy a new ticket.'

Nell stares at her ticket, which the woman is holding towards her. And it is there in black and white. NON-TRANSFERABLE. 'A new ticket? How much is it?'

The woman says something, then puts her hand over the receiver. 'One hundred and seventy-eight euros. You want to book it?'

A hundred and seventy-eight euros. About a hundred and fifty pounds. 'Uh – um – You know what? I . . . I just have to work something out.'

She dare not look at the woman's face as she takes the ticket back from her. She feels like a fool. Of course a cheap ticket would be non-transferable. 'Thank you so much.' She bolts for the safety of her room, ignoring the woman, who is calling after her.

*

Nell sits on the end of the bed and swears softly to herself. So, she can either pay half a week's wages to get home, or carry on alone with the World's Worst Romantic Weekend for one more night. She can hide in this attic room with its French television that she can't understand. She can sit by herself in cafés, trying not to look at the happy couples.

She decides to make herself a coffee, but there is no kettle in the room.

'Oh, for God's sake,' she says aloud. She decides she hates Paris.

And it is then that she sees a half-open envelope on the floor, half under the bed, with something sticking out from it. She bends down and picks it up. It is two tickets to a show by an artist she has vaguely heard of. She turns it over. They must have belonged to the American woman. She puts them down. She'll decide what to do with them later. For now she needs to put on some make-up, brush her hair, and then she really needs to get a coffee.

Outside in the daylight she feels more cheerful about Paris. She walks until she sees a café she likes the look of, and orders a coffee and a croissant. She sits out on the street, huddled

39

against the cold, beside several other people who are doing the same thing.

The coffee is good and the croissant is delicious. She makes a note of the café's name in her book, in case she wants to come back. She leaves a tip and walks back to the hotel, thinking, 'Well, I've had worse breakfasts'. An elderly Frenchman tips his hat to her, and a little dog stops to say hello. Across the road there is a handbag shop, and she gazes in through the window at some of the most beautiful bags she has ever seen. The shop looks like a film set.

She cannot work out what to do. She walks slowly, debating with herself, scribbling her reasons for and against taking the five o'clock train, into her little notebook. If she got that train, she could actually make the late train down to Brighton and surprise the girls. She could save this weekend. She could get blind drunk and they would look after her. That was what girlfriends were for.

But the thought of spending another hundred and fifty pounds on an already disastrous weekend makes her heart sink. And she does not want her first trip to Paris to end with her running away, tail between her legs. She does not want to remember the first time she went to Paris as the time she got dumped and ran home without even seeing the Eiffel Tower.

She is still thinking when she arrives at the hotel, so she almost forgets until she reaches into her pocket for the key. And pulls out the American woman's tickets.

'Excuse me?' she says to the receptionist. 'Do you know what happened to the woman who was sharing my room? Room forty-two?'

The woman flicks through a sheaf of papers. 'She checked out first thing this morning. A . . . family emergency, I believe.' Her face reveals nothing. 'There are many such emergencies this weekend.'

'She left some tickets in the room. For an artist's show. I was wondering what to do with them.'

She holds them out and the receptionist studies them.

'She went straight to the airport . . . Oh. This is a very popular show, I think. It was on the news last night. People are queuing for many hours to see it.'

Nell looks at the tickets again.

'I would go to this exhibition, Mademoiselle.' The woman smiles at her. 'If you can . . . if your family emergency can wait.'

Nell gazes at the tickets. 'Maybe I will.'

'Mademoiselle?'

Nell turns back to her.

'We will not be charging you for the room, if you choose to stay tonight. To make up for the inconvenience.' She smiles in apology.

'Oh. Thank you,' Nell says, surprised.

And she decides. It is just one more night. She will stay.

Chapter Seven

Sandrine, Fabien's ex-girlfriend, always said he got up too late. Now, standing near the end of a queue that is marked with signs saying 'One hour from this point', 'Two hours from this point', Fabien kicks himself for not getting up at eight o'clock as he had planned.

He was meant to visit his father, to help him put up some shelves. But somehow, as he rode his bike beside the river, he had seen the signs and stopped. He had stood at the end cheerfully some forty-five minutes ago, thinking the queue would move quickly. But he has moved forward just some ten feet. It is a cold, clear afternoon and he is starting to feel the chill. He pulls his woollen beanie further over his head and kicks the ground with the toes of his boots.

He could just quit the queue, head off and meet his father as he had said he would. He could go home and tidy up the apartment. He could put more oil in his moped and check the tyres. He could do the paperwork he had

43

put off doing for months. But nobody else has ducked out of the queue, and neither does he.

Somehow, he thinks, he might feel better if he stays. He will have achieved something today. He will not have given up, like Sandrine says he always does.

It is, of course, nothing to do with the fact that Frida Kahlo is Sandrine's favourite artist. He pulls up his collar, picturing himself bumping into her at the bar. 'Oh, yes,' he would say casually. 'I just went to see the Diego Rivera and Frida Kahlo exhibition.' She would look surprised, maybe even pleased. Perhaps he will buy the catalogue and give it to her.

Even as he thinks about it, he knows it is a stupid idea. Sandrine is not going to be anywhere near the bar where he works. She has avoided it since they split up. What is he doing here anyway?

He looks up to see a girl walking slowly towards the end of the long line of people, her navy hat pulled low over her fringe. Her face wears the look of shock he sees on everyone else's when they see how long the queue is.

She stops near a woman a few people down from him. In her hand she holds two slips of paper. 'Excuse me? Do you speak English? Is this the queue for the Kahlo exhibition?'

44

She is not the first to ask. The woman shrugs, and says something in Spanish. Fabien sees what she is holding and steps forward. 'But you have tickets,' he says. 'You do not need to queue here.' He points towards the front of the queue. 'Look – if you have tickets the queue is there.'

'Oh.' She smiles. 'Thank you. That's a relief!'

And then he recognizes her. 'You were at Café des Bastides last night?'

She looks a little startled. Then her hand goes to her mouth. 'Oh. The waiter. I spilled wine all over you. I'm so sorry.'

'*De rien*,' he says. 'It's nothing.'

'Sorry, anyway. And . . . thanks.'

She makes as if to walk away, then turns and gazes at him, and then at the people on each side of him. She seems to be thinking. 'You're waiting for someone?' she asks Fabien.

'No.'

'Would you . . . would you like my other ticket? I have two.'

'You don't need it?'

'They were . . . a gift. I have no use for the other one.'

He stares at the girl, waiting for her to explain, but she says no more. He holds out a hand and takes the offered ticket. 'Thank you!'

'It's the least I can do.'

They walk beside each other to the small queue at the front, where tickets are being checked. He can't stop grinning at this unexpected gift. Her gaze slides towards him and she smiles. He notices her ears have gone pink.

'So,' he says. 'You are here for a holiday?'

'Just the weekend,' she says. 'Just – you know – fancied a trip.'

He tilts his head sideways. 'It's good. To just go. Very . . .' he searches for the word '. . . *impulsif*.'

She shakes her head. 'You . . . work in the restaurant every day?'

'Most days. I want to be a writer.' He looks down and kicks at a pebble. 'But I think maybe I will always be a waiter.'

'Oh, no,' she says, her voice suddenly clear and strong. 'I'm sure you'll get there. You have all that going on in front of you. People's lives, I mean. In the restaurant. I'm sure you must be full of ideas.'

He shrugs. 'It's . . . a dream. I'm not sure it's a good one.'

And then they are at the front and the security guard steers her towards the counter to have her bag searched. Fabien sees she feels awkward and does not know if he should wait.

But as he stands there, she lifts a hand as if

to say goodbye. 'Well, thank you,' she says. 'I hope you enjoy the exhibition.'

He pushes his hands deeper in his pockets, and nods. 'Goodbye.'

He doesn't even know her name. And then she heads down the stairs, and disappears into the crowd.

For months Fabien has been stuck in a groove, unable to think of anything but Sandrine. Every bar he has been to reminds him of somewhere they had been. Every song he hears reminds him of her, of the shape of her top lip, the scent of her hair. It has been like living with a ghost.

But now, inside the gallery, something happens to him. He finds he is gripped by the paintings, the huge colourful canvases by Diego Rivera, the tiny, agonized self-portraits by Frida Kahlo the woman Rivera loved. Fabien barely notices the crowds that cluster in front of the pictures.

He stops in front of a perfect little painting in which she has pictured her spine as a cracked column. There is something about the grief in her eyes that won't let him look away. *That* is suffering, he thinks. Not the loss of Sandrine who, by the end, only ever seemed to criticize him anyway. Fabien feels as if a weight has lifted.

He finds himself standing again and again in front of the same pictures, reading about the couple's life, the passion they shared for their art, for workers' rights, for each other. He wants to live like these people. He has to be a writer. He has to.

He is filled with an urge to go home and write something that is fresh and new, and has in it the honesty of these pictures. Most of all he just wants to write. But what?

And then he sees her, standing in front of the girl with the broken column for a spine. Her gaze locked on the girl in the painting, her eyes wide and sad. Her navy hat is clutched in her right hand. As he watches, a tear slides down her cheek. Her left hand lifts and, without looking away from the picture, she wipes it away with her palm. She looks over suddenly, perhaps feeling his gaze on her, and their eyes meet. Almost before he knows what he is doing, Fabien steps forward.

'I never . . . I never got a chance to ask you,' he says. 'Would you like to go for coffee?'

Chapter Eight

The Café Cheval Bleu is packed at four o'clock in the afternoon, but the waitress finds Fabien a table inside. Nell has the feeling he is one of those men who always gets a good table inside. He orders a tiny black coffee, and she says, 'For me too,' because she does not want him to hear her terrible French accent.

There is a short, awkward silence.

'It was a good exhibition, yes?'

'I don't normally cry at pictures,' she says. 'I feel a bit silly now I'm out here.'

'No. No, it was very moving. And the crowds, and the people, and the photographs . . .'

He starts to talk about the exhibition. He says he had known about the artist's work, but had not realised that he would be so moved by it. 'I feel it here, you know?' he said, thumping his chest. 'So . . . powerful.'

'Yes,' she says.

Nobody she knows talks like this. They talk about what Tessa wore to work, or *Coronation*

Street, or who fell over when they were blind drunk last weekend.

'I think . . . I want to write like they paint. Does that make sense? I want someone to read and feel it like *bouf!*'

She can't help smiling.

'You think it's funny?' He looks hurt.

'Oh, no. It was the way you said *bouf*.'

'*Bouf?*'

'It's not a word we have in England. It just – I –' She shakes her head. 'It's just a funny word. *Bouf*.'

He stares at her for a minute, then lets out a great laugh. '*Bouf!*'

And the ice is broken. The coffee arrives, and she stirs two sugars into it so that she will not make a face drinking it.

Fabien swallows his in two gulps. 'So how do you find Paris, Nell-from-England?'

'I like it. What I've seen. But I haven't been to any of the tourist places. I haven't seen the Eiffel Tower or Notre Dame or that bridge where all the lovers attach little padlocks. I don't think I'll really have time now.'

'You will come back. People always do. What are you going to do this evening?'

'I don't know. Maybe find another place to eat. Maybe just flop at the hotel. I'm quite tired.' She laughed. 'Are you working at the restaurant?'

'No. Not tonight.'

She tries not to look disappointed.

He glances down at his watch. '*Merde*! I promised my father I would help him with something. I have to go.' He looks up. 'But I am meeting some friends at a bar later this evening. You would be welcome to join us, if you like.'

'Oh. You're very kind, but –'

'You cannot spend your evening in Paris in your hotel room.'

'Really. I'll be fine.'

She hears her mother's voice: *You don't just go out with strange men.* He could be anyone. He has a shaven head.

'Nell. Please let me buy you one drink. Just to say thank you for the ticket.'

'I don't know . . .'

He has the most amazing grin. She feels herself wobble. 'Is it far?'

'Nowhere is far.' He laughs. 'You are in Paris!'

'OK. Where shall we meet?'

'I'll pick you up. Where is your hotel?'

She tells him and says, 'So where are we going?'

'Where the night takes us. You are the Impulsive Girl from England, after all!' He salutes and

51

then he is gone, kick-starting his moped and roaring away down the road.

Nell lets herself back into her room, her mind still buzzing with the afternoon's events. She sees the paintings in the gallery, Fabien's large hands around the little coffee cup, the sad eyes of the tiny woman in the painting. She sees the gardens beside the river, wide and open and the River Seine flowing beyond them. She hears the hiss of the doors opening and closing on the underground. She feels like every bit of her is fizzing. She feels like someone out of a book.

She has a shower and washes her hair. She sorts through the few clothes she brought with her and wonders whether any of them are Parisian enough. Everyone here is so stylish. They do not dress like each other. They do not dress like English girls.

Almost without thinking, she races downstairs to the little row of shops she had passed earlier. She stops in front of a window. She had noticed the green dress with the pineapples this morning. It had made her think of 1950s film stars. She takes a breath and pushes the door open.

Twenty minutes later she is back in her hotel

room, with a carrier-bag. She takes out the dress and puts it on. She stands in front of the mirror, looking at its lovely folds, the way it nips in at the waist, and she realizes that she has not thought about Pete for the entire afternoon. She is in Paris, wearing a dress she bought in a Paris shop, getting ready to go out with a strange man she picked up in a gallery!

She pulls her hair back into a loose knot, puts on her lipstick, sits down on the bed and laughs.

Twenty minutes later she is still sitting on the bed, staring into space.

She is in Paris, getting ready to go out with a strange man she has picked up in a gallery.

She must be insane.

This is the stupidest thing she has ever done in her life.

This is more stupid than buying an expensive dress with pineapples on it.

This is even more stupid than buying a ticket to Paris for a man who had told her he couldn't decide if her face looked more like a horse or a currant bun.

She will be in a newspaper headline or, worse, in one of those tiny news stories that aren't important enough to be a headline.

**Girl found dead in Paris after
boyfriend fails to show up.
'I told her not to go out with
strange men,' says mother.**

She gazes at herself in the mirror. This is
madness. What has she done?

Nell grabs her key, slips into her shoes and
runs down the narrow staircase to Reception.
The receptionist is there, and Nell waits for her
to come off the phone before she leans over,
and says quietly, 'If a man comes for me, will
you tell him I am ill?'

The woman frowns. 'Not a family emergency?'

'No. I – er – I have a stomach ache.'

'A stomach ache. I'm so sorry, Mademoiselle.
And what does this man look like?'

'Very short hair. Rides a moped. Obviously
not in here. I . . . He's tall. Nice eyes.'

'Nice eyes.'

'Look, he's the only man likely to come in
here asking for me.'

The receptionist nods as if this is a fair point.

'I – he wants me to go out this evening
and . . . it's not a good idea.'

'So . . . you don't like him.'

'Oh, no, he's lovely. It's just, well – I don't
really know him.'

54

'But . . . how will you know him if you don't go out with him?'

'I don't know him well enough to go out in a strange city to a place I don't know. Possibly with other people I don't know.'

'That's a lot of don't-knows.'

'Exactly.'

'So you will be staying in your room tonight.'

'Yes. No. I don't know.' She stands there, hearing how silly she sounds.

The woman looks her slowly up and down. 'It's a very nice dress.'

'Oh. Thank you.'

'What a pity. Your stomach ache. Still.' She smiles, turns back to her paperwork. 'Maybe some other time.'

Nell sits in her room, watching French television. A man is talking to another man. One of them shakes his head so hard his chins wobble in slow motion. She looks at the clock often as it ticks slowly round to eight o'clock. Her stomach rumbles. She remembers Fabien saying something about a little falafel stall in the Jewish quarter. She wonders what it would have felt like on the back of that moped.

She pulls out her notebook and grabs the hotel biro from the bedside table. She writes:

REASONS I AM RIGHT TO STAY
IN TONIGHT

1. He might be an axe murderer.
2. He will probably want sex.
3. Perhaps both 1 and 2.
4. I may end up in a part of Paris I don't know.
5. I may have to talk to taxi drivers.
6. I may have problems getting back into the hotel late at night.
7. My dress is silly.
8. I will have to pretend to be impulsive.
9. I will have to speak French or eat French food in front of French people.
10. If I go to bed early, I will be up nice and early for the train home.

She sits there, staring at her neat list for some time. Then on the other side of the page she writes:

1. I am in Paris.

She stares at it a bit longer. Then, as the clock strikes eight, she shoves the notebook back into her bag, grabs her coat and runs down the narrow staircase towards Reception.

He is there, leaning on the desk and talking to the receptionist, and at the sight of him she feels the colour flood into her cheeks. As she walks towards them, her heart beating fast, she is trying to work out how to explain herself. Whatever she says will sound stupid. It will be clear that she was afraid of going out with him.

'Ah, Mademoiselle. I was just telling your friend here that I thought you might take a few minutes.'

'You are ready to go?' Fabien is smiling. She cannot remember the last time someone looked so pleased to see her – except her cousin's dog, when he tried to do something quite rude to her leg.

'If you return after midnight, Mademoiselle, you will need to use this code at the main door.' The receptionist hands her a small card. 'I am so glad your stomach ache is better.'

'You have stomach ache?' Fabien says, as he hands her a spare helmet.

The Paris night is crisp and cold. She has never been on a bike before. She remembers reading about how many people die while riding bikes. But the helmet is already on her head and he is shifting forward on his seat, motioning for her to get on behind.

'I'm fine now,' she says.

Please don't let me die, she thinks.

'Good! First we will drink, and then maybe we eat, but first we show you some of Paris, yes?' And as she wraps her arms around his waist the little moped leaps forward into the night and, with a squeal, they are off.

Chapter Nine

Fabien whizzes down the Rue de Rivoli, dipping in and out of the traffic, feeling the girl's hands tighten around his waist whenever he speeds up. At the traffic lights he stops and asks, 'You OK?' His voice is muffled through his helmet,

She is smiling, her nose tipped red. 'Yes!' she says, and he finds he is grinning too. Sandrine always looked blankly at him on the moped, as if she were hiding her thoughts about the way he drove. The English girl squeals and laughs and sometimes, when he swerves to avoid a car that pulls out of a side street, she yells, 'Oh my God, oh my God, oh my God!'

He takes her down crowded avenues, through back streets, whizzing over a bridge, so that she can see the river glittering beneath them. Then they go round onto another bridge, so she can see the cathedral of Notre Dame lit up in the darkness, its stone monsters gazing down at them with shadowed faces.

Then, before she can breathe, they are riding

along Paris's main street, the Champs-Élysées, weaving through the cars, beeping at pedestrians who step out into the road. There, he slows and points upwards, so that she can see . . . He feels her lean back a little as they drive past. He puts his thumb up and she puts her own up in response.

He speeds over a bridge, and turns right along the river. He dodges the buses and taxis and ignores the horns of drivers, until he sees the spot he wants. He slows and cuts the engine by the main path. Tourist boats float along the river with their bright lights, and there are stalls selling Eiffel Tower key-rings and candy floss. Then there it is. The Tower soars above them, a million pieces of iron pointing into the black sky.

She releases her grip on his jacket and gets off his bike carefully, as if during the journey her legs have become stiff. She pulls off her helmet. He notices that she does not bother to fix her hair, as Sandrine would have done. She is too busy gazing upwards, her mouth an O of surprise.

He pulls off his own helmet, leans forward over the handlebars.

'There! Now you can say you have seen all of Paris's finest sights – and in . . . uh . . . twenty-two minutes.'

She turns and looks at him, her eyes glittering. 'That,' she says, 'was the most bloody terrifying and absolutely best thing I have ever done in my entire life.'

He laughs.

'It's the Eiffel Tower!'

'You want to go up? We will probably have to queue.'

She thinks for a moment. 'I think we've done enough queuing for today. What I would really like is a stiff drink.'

'A what drink?'

'Wine!' she says, and climbs back onto the moped. 'Give me wine!'

He feels her hands slide around his waist as he starts up the engine and drives into the night.

An hour later they are drinking in a bar. There was a mention of food some time ago but it seems to have been forgotten. She has relaxed in here, with Emil and Sasha and that friend of Emil with the red hair whose name Fabien never can remember. She has taken off her hat and her coat and her hair swings around her face as she laughs. Everyone speaks in English for her, but Emil is trying to teach her to swear in French.

'*Merde!*' he is saying. 'But you have to pull the face too. *Merde!*'

'*Merde!*' She throws up her hands, like Emil, then bursts out laughing again. 'I can't do the accent.'

'*Sheet.*'

'*Sheet,*' she says, copying his deep voice. 'I can do that one.'

'But you don't swear like you mean it. I thought all English girls cursed like sailors, no?'

'*Bouf!*' she says, and swings round to look at Fabien.

He finds he keeps watching her. Not beautiful, not in the way Sandrine was beautiful. But there is something about her face that keeps you looking: the way she screws up her nose when she laughs. The way she looks a little guilty when she does that, as if she is doing something she shouldn't. Her smile, wide, with tiny white child's teeth.

They lock eyes for a moment and he sees a question, and an answer between them. Emil is fun, the look says, but we both know that this is about us. When he looks away, he feels a little knot of something in his belly. He goes up to the bar, orders another round of drinks.

'You finally moved on, uh?' says Fred, behind the bar.

'She's just a friend. Visiting from England.'

'If you say so,' Fred says, and lines up the drinks. He doesn't need to ask what they want. It's Saturday night. 'I saw her, by the way.'

'Sandrine?'

'Yes. She said she has a new job. Something to do with a design studio.'

He feels a brief pang that something so major has happened in her life without him knowing.

'It's good,' Fred says, without meeting his eye, 'that you are moving on.'

And in that one sentence, Fabien realizes that Sandrine has someone else. *It's good that you are moving on.*

As he carries the drinks towards the table, it hits him. It's a pang of discomfort, not of pain. It doesn't matter. It's time to let her go.

'I thought you were getting wine,' Nell says, her eyes widening, as he arrives with the drinks.

'It's time for tequila,' he says. 'Just one. Just – because.'

'Because you are in Paris and it's Saturday night,' says Emil. 'And who needs an excuse for tequila?'

He sees a flash of doubt on her face. But then she lifts her chin. 'Let's do it,' she says. She sucks the lime, then downs the contents of the little glass, screwing her eyes shut with a shudder. 'Oh my God.'

'Now we *know* it's Saturday night,' says Emil. 'Let's party! Are we going on later?'

Fabien wants to. He feels alive and reckless. He wants to see Nell laughing until the small hours. He wants to go to a club and dance with her, one hand on her sweaty back, her eyes locked on his. He wants to be awake in the early hours for the right reasons, alive with the drink and the fun and the streets of Paris. He wants to bathe in the sense of hope that comes with someone new, someone who sees in you only the best of everything, not the worst. 'Sure. If Nell wants to.'

'Nell,' says Emil. 'What kind of name is this? It's a normal English name?'

'It's the worst name ever,' she says. 'My mother named me after someone in one of Charles Dickens's books.'

'It could have been worse. You could have been – what is her name? – Miss Havisham.'

'Mercy Pecksniff.'

'Fanny Dorrit.' They are all laughing.

She claps a hand over her mouth, giggling. 'How do you all know so much about Dickens?'

'We read too much. Fabien reads all the time. It's terrible. We have to fight to get him to come out.' Emil lifts a glass. 'He is like a – a – How do you say it? A hermit. He is a hermit.

I have no idea how you got him out tonight, but I am very happy. *Salut!'*

'*Salut!*' she says, and then she reaches into her pocket for her phone, and stares at it. She looks shocked and peers closer, as if checking she has read correctly.

'Everything is OK?' Fabien says, when she says nothing.

'Fine,' she says, but she is distracted. She fiddles with the edge of her scarf. 'Actually . . .' she says. 'No. I think I need to go. I'm really sorry.'

'Go?' says Emil. 'You cannot go, Nell! The night is just beginning!'

She looks stunned. 'I'm – I'm really sorry. Something has . . .' She is reaching for her bag and coat. She stands, and begins to make her way towards Fabien. He gets up to let her pass. 'I'm sorry. Something has – someone has turned up to see me. I have to –'

He looks down at her, and he can see it on her face. 'You have a boyfriend.'

'Sort of. Yes.' She bites her lip.

He is shocked by how disappointed he feels. 'He has turned up at the hotel.'

'You want me to take you?'

'Oh, no. I think I can walk it from here.'

They go to the door. 'OK. You walk down to

the church there, then turn left, and you are on the road of your hotel.'

She cannot meet his eye. Finally she looks up. 'I'm really sorry,' she said. 'I had such a great time. Thank you.'

He shrugs. '*De rien.*'

'It was nothing,' she translates.

But it was something. He realizes he cannot ask for her number. Not now. He raises a hand. She looks at him once more. Then, almost reluctantly, she turns away, and she is off, half walking, half running down the street towards the church, her bag flying out behind her.

'You said she was impulsive,' said Emil, appearing behind him. 'But . . . what happened? Was it something I said?'

Chapter Ten

He is waiting in Reception. He sits, legs apart, arms wide along the back of the sofa, and doesn't get up when he sees her. 'Babe!'

She is frozen. She glances at the receptionist, who is looking very hard at some paperwork.

'Surprise!'

'What are you doing here?'

'I thought we could turn your weekend in Paris into one night in Paris. Still counts, right?'

She stands in the middle of the reception area. 'But you said you weren't coming.'

'You know me. Full of surprises. Hotel looks nice.'

It's like she is looking at a stranger. His hair is too long, and his faded jeans and desert boots, which she had thought were so cool, just look tacky and tired.

Stop it, she tells herself. He has come all this way. He has done the very thing she wanted him to do. That must count for something.

'You look gorgeous. Do I get a welcome?'

She steps forward, kisses him. He tastes of tobacco. 'Sorry. I – I'm just a bit shocked.'

'I like to keep you on your toes, eh? So, shall we dump my stuff and get a drink? Or we could spend the evening upstairs with a bit of room service?' He grins and lifts an eyebrow. Nell sees the receptionist out of the corner of her eye. She is looking at him in the way she would look at something nasty a guest had trodden into her hallway.

He hasn't shaved, she thinks. He hasn't even shaved.

'They don't do room service here. Only breakfast.'

He shrugs and rises from his seat. 'Top dress, by the way. Very . . . chic.'

'Just one thing,' she says. 'I just – I just want to know – how did you end up coming after all? You said you weren't going to make it. That's what the text said.'

'Well . . . I didn't like to leave you here alone. I know how anxious you get about stuff. Especially when plans change and that.'

'But you were fine leaving me alone last night.'

He looks awkward. 'Yes. Well.'

There is a long silence.

'Well . . . what?'

He scratches his head, smiles his charming smile. 'All right. Well, Trish got in touch and said she was a bit worried about you.'

'Trish rang you?'

'She texted me. She said she couldn't get hold of you and she wanted to make sure everything was OK.'

Nell is rooted to the floor. 'What did she say?'

'Does it matter? Look, I'm here now. Let's enjoy it, shall we? Come on, we've only got till tomorrow. And this ticket cost me a small fortune.'

She stares at him. He holds out his hand. Almost reluctantly, she hands him the key and he turns and begins to walk up the stairs, his bag slung over his back.

'Mademoiselle.'

Nell turns, in a daze. She had forgotten the receptionist was there.

'Your friend left a message.'

'Fabien?' She fails to keep the eagerness from her voice.

'No. A woman. While you were out.'

She hands over a piece of hotel headed paper.

PETE IS ON HIS WAY. HAVE KICKED HIS ARSE. SORRY, WE HAD NO IDEA. HOPE WEEKEND STILL WORKS OUT OK. TRISH

69

She stares at the note, gazes towards the stair-well, and then she turns back to the recep-tionist. She stuffs the piece of paper deep into her pocket.

'Could you tell me the best place to get a taxi?' she says.

'With pleasure,' says the receptionist.

She has forty euros in her pocket and she throws twenty at the driver, then leaps out, not caring about the change.

The bar is a dark mass of bodies, bottles and low lights. She pushes her way through, scan-ning the faces for someone she knows, her nostrils filled with the smells of sweat and perfume. The table they had been sitting at is filled with people she does not recognize. He is nowhere to be seen.

She goes upstairs, where it is quieter and people sit chatting on sofas, but he is not there either. She fights her way back down the stairs to the bar where she was served.

'Excuse me!' She has to wait to get the atten-tion of the barman. 'Hello! My friend who was here. Have you seen him?'

The barman squints, then nods as if he remembers. 'Fabien?'

'Yes. Yes!' Of course they all knew him.

'He is gone.'

She feels her stomach drop. She has missed him. That's it. The barman leans across to pour someone a drink.

'*Merde*,' she says softly. She feels hollow with disappointment.

The barman appears beside her, a drink in his hand. 'You could try the Wildcat. That's where he and Emil usually end up.'

'The Wildcat? Where is that?'

'Rue des Gentilhommes des –' His voice is drowned in a burst of laughter, and he turns away, leaning across to hear someone else's order.

Nell runs out onto the street. She stops a taxi.

'Emergency!' she says.

The driver, an Asian man, looks up into his mirror, waiting.

'Wildcat,' she says. 'Rue des Gentilhommes something. Please tell me you know it.'

He turns in his seat. '*Que?*'

'Wildcat. Bar. Club. Wild. Cat.'

Her voice lifts. He shakes his head. Nell puts her face into her hands, thinking. Then she winds down her window and yells at three young men on the pavement outside the bar. 'Excuse me! You know the Wildcat? Wildcat Bar?'

One nods, lifts his chin. 'You want to take us?'

She scans their faces – drunk, cheerful, open – and she makes a judgement.

'Sure, if you know it. Where is it?'

'We show you!'

The young men jump in, all drunken smiles and handshakes. She declines the offer to sit on the lap of the short one, and accepts a mint from the one in the middle. She is squashed between them, breathing in the smell of alcohol and cigarette smoke.

'It's a good club. You know it?' The man who first spoke to her leans across and shakes her hand cheerfully.

'No,' she says. And as he tells the taxi driver where to go, she leans back in a car full of strangers and waits to see where she will end up next.

Chapter Eleven

'One more drink. Ah, come on. It's just getting good.' Emil claps a hand on his shoulder.

'I'm not really in the mood.'

'You were in the mood. Come on. We will go on to Pierre's. He said he's got a whole bunch of people coming over. Party!'

'Thanks, Emil, but I'll finish this beer and go. Work tomorrow. You know.'

Emil shrugs, lifts his own bottle, then turns back to the girl he has been talking to.

It was bound to happen. Fabien watches Emil laughing with the redhead. He has liked her for ages, but he is not sure how much she likes him back. Emil is not unhappy, though. He just bounces onto the next thing, like a puppy. *Hey! Let's have fun!*

Don't knock it, Fabien scolds himself. Better than being a loser like you.

He feels a faint dread at what will come next. The long evenings at his flat. The work on the book that he is no longer sure is worth working on. The disappointment because Nell disappeared. The way he will kick himself for thinking it was going to be something more. He can't blame her – he never even asked if she had a boyfriend. Of course a girl like her would have a boyfriend.

He feels his mood sinking and knows it is time to go home. He does not want to depress anyone else. He claps Emil on the shoulder, nods goodbye to the others, and pulls his hat lower over his ears. Outside he climbs onto his moped, wondering if he should be driving at all after all he has had to drink.

He kick-starts the little bike and pulls out onto the street.

He has stopped at the end of the road to adjust his jacket when he hears Emil's loud whistle. He turns.

Emil is standing on the pavement beside a crowd of people. He is pointing at someone, and waving for him to return.

Fabien recognizes the tilt of her head, the way she stands, one heel lifted. He sits for a moment. Then, a smile breaking over his face, he turns his bike and rides back to her.

*

It is two thirty in the morning. Fabien has drunk more than he has drunk in weeks. His sides hurt from laughing. The Wildcat is heaving with people. One of Fabien's favourite tracks comes on, which he had played in the restaurant during clean-up time until the boss had banned it. Emil, who is in crazy party mode, leaps onto the bar and starts dancing, pointing at his chest and grinning at the people below him. A cheer goes up.

Fabien feels Nell's fingers resting on his arm and takes her hand. She is laughing, her hair sweaty, with strands stuck to her face. She took off her coat some time ago and he suspects they may not find it again. They have been dancing for hours.

The red-headed girl gets up on the bar beside Emil, helped by a sea of hands, and starts dancing. They shimmy together, swigging from bottles of beer. The barmen stand back, watching. It is not the first time the bar of the Wildcat has become a dance floor and it will not be the last.

Nell is trying to say something to him.

He stoops lower to hear her.

'I've never danced on a bar,' she says.

'No? Do it!' he says.

She laughs, shakes her head, and he holds her gaze. And it is as if she remembers something. She reaches a hand to his shoulder, and he helps her up, and there she is, above him, dancing. Emil lifts a bottle in salute, and she is off, locked into the rhythm, her eyes closed, hair swinging. She wipes sweat from her face and swigs from a bottle. Two, then three more people join them up there.

Fabien is not tempted. He just wants to stand here, feeling the music vibrate through him, part of the crowd, watching her, enjoying her pleasure, knowing he is part of it.

She opens her eyes then, searching him out among the sea of faces. She spots him and smiles, and Fabien realizes he is feeling something he thought he had forgotten how to feel.

He is happy.

Chapter Twelve

They are walking arm in arm through the deserted streets, past art galleries and huge old buildings. It is a quarter to four in the morning. Her legs ache from the dancing, and her ears are still ringing, and she thinks she has never felt less tired in her life.

When they left the Wildcat they had swayed a little, drunk on the evening, beer, tequila and life, but somehow in the last half-hour she has sobered.

'Nell, I have no idea where we are going.'

She doesn't care. She could walk like this for ever. 'Well, I can't go back to the hotel. Pete might still be there.'

He nudges her. 'You shared with the American woman. Maybe he's not so bad.'

'I'd rather share with the American. Even with the snoring.'

She has told him the whole story. At first Fabien had looked like he wanted to hit Pete.

She realized, with shame, that she quite liked that.

'Now I feel a little bit sorry for Pete,' says Fabien. 'He comes all the way to Paris to find you, and you run away with a Frenchman.'

Nell grins. 'I don't feel bad about it. Isn't that awful?'

'You are clearly a very cruel woman.'

She huddles closer to him. 'Oh. Horrible.'

He puts his arm around her. She lost her coat in the club, and she is wearing his jacket. He had assured her he did not feel the cold. She didn't either, really, but she liked wearing his jacket.

'You know, Nell, you can stay with me. If you like.'

She hears her mother suddenly. *You go back to a strange man's house? In Paris?*

'That would be lovely. But I'm not going to sleep with you.'

Her words hang in the night air.

'I'm disappointed, Nell-from-England, but I understand. It is the duty of a cruel woman to crush a man's hopes and dreams.' He pulls down the corners of his mouth, an expression that seems purely French to her. And then he grins.

'Where is your flat?'

'It's a studio. Not smart, like your hotel. Maybe ten minutes' walk.'

She has no idea what will happen next. It is absolutely thrilling.

Fabien lives at the top of a narrow block that looks over a courtyard. The stairs are lined with cream stone and smell of old wood and polish. They walk up in silence. He has warned her that elderly women live in the other apartments. If he makes any noise after ten p.m. they will rap on his door early in the morning to complain. He does not mind, though, he tells her. His apartment is cheap because the owner is too lazy to update it. Sandrine hated it, he tells her.

As they reach the top of the stairs she steels herself. Trish once dated a man and, when she went back to his flat, had found shelves full of books about murderers.

He opens the door and ushers her in. She stops on the threshold and stares.

Fabien's flat is one big room, with one large window looking out over the rooftops. A desk is covered with piles of paper. A sofa-bed sits in the corner, and a large mirror on the other side. The floor is wood. It might have been painted a long time ago, but is now pale and colourless. There is a large bed at one end, a small sofa against a wall, and the third wall is covered with pictures cut from magazines.

'Oh,' he says, when he sees her looking. 'I did that when I was a student. I am too lazy to take it down.'

Everything – the desk, the chairs, the pictures – is strange and interesting. She walks around, gazing at a stuffed crow on a shelf, the workshop light that hangs from the ceiling, the collection of pebbles by the bathroom door. The television is a tiny box that looks twenty years old. There are six glasses on the mantelpiece and a stack of plates.

He runs his hand over his head. 'It's a mess. I was not expecting –'

'It's beautiful. It's . . . it's magical.'

'Magical?'

'I just . . . like it. How you put things together. Everything looks like it's a story.'

He blinks at her, as if he is seeing his home through different eyes.

'Excuse me for a moment,' he says. 'I just need . . .' He motions to the bathroom.

It is probably a good thing. She feels reckless, like someone she doesn't know. She peels off his jacket, straightening her dress, and walks slowly around the room until she is gazing out of the window. The rooftops of Paris, dark and moonlit, are like a promise.

She looks down at the pile of hand-written pages. Some are dirty, marked with the treads of people's shoes. She picks one up and starts to scan it for words she knows.

When he finally comes out of the bathroom, she is holding her fourth page and sorting through the pile for the fifth.

'Read it to me,' she says.

'No. It's no good. I don't want to read this –'

'Just these pages. Please. So I can say, "When I was in Paris a real writer read to me from his own work." It's part of my Paris adventure.'

He looks at her as if he cannot say 'no' to her. She puts on her best pleading face.

'I have not shown it to anyone.'

She pats the sofa next to her. 'Maybe it's time you did.'

Some time later he drops page twelve on the floor.

'You can't stop.'

'The pages are missing. Anyway – like I said, it's no good.'

'But you can't stop. You have to remember what you wrote, and send it off to a publisher. It's really good. You have to be a writer. Well, you *are* a writer. Just not a published one, yet.'

He shakes his head.

'You *are*. It's – it's lovely. I think it's . . . the way you write about the woman. About how she feels, the way she sees things. I saw myself in her. She's . . .'

He looks at her, surprised. Almost without knowing what she is doing she leans forward, takes his face in her hands and kisses him. She is in Paris, in the apartment of a man she does not know, and she has never done anything that felt more sensible in her life. His arms close round her and she feels herself being pulled into him.

'You are . . . beautiful, Nell.'

'And everything you say sounds better because it's in French. I might just have to speak in a fake French accent for the rest of my life.'

He pours them each a glass of wine, and they sit, gaze at each other and grin. They talk about work and their parents, their knees touching, leaning against each other on the little sofa. He tells her that this evening has released him from Sandrine. She talks about Pete, and giggles when she thinks about him reaching the room and turning back to find she is not there. They imagine the American woman turning up at the room now, when Pete is there, and giggle some more.

At some point she goes to the loo and stares at herself in the mirror. She is grey with tiredness. Her hair is all over the place, her eye make-up has rubbed off. And yet she glows; she looks full of mischief and joy.

When she comes back, he is reading her book.

She stops. 'What are you doing?'

'What is this?' He holds out the list.

REASONS I AM RIGHT TO STAY IN TONIGHT.

'I am an axe murderer? I might want to have sex with you?'

He is laughing, but he is a little shocked too.

'Oh, God. I didn't mean for you to see that.' She has blushed to her ears.

'It fell out of your bag. I was just putting it back in. "Have to pretend to be impulsive".' He looks up at her, surprised.

She is filled with misery. 'OK. I'm not the person you think I am. Or at least I wasn't. I'm not impulsive. I nearly didn't come tonight, because even the thought of taxi drivers scared

83

me. I let you think I was a different kind of person. I'm . . . I'm sorry.'

He studies the list, and then he looks up again. He is half laughing. 'Who says you are a different kind of person?'

She waits.

'Was it somebody else dancing on that bar? Chasing me around Paris in a taxi with strange men? Leaving her boyfriend in a hotel room without even telling him she was going?'

He reaches out a hand, and she takes it. She lets him pull her to him. She sits astride his lap and studies his lovely, kind face.

'I think you are exactly this woman, Nell-from-England. You are whoever you choose to be.'

It is getting light outside. She is light-headed with drink and tiredness. They kiss again, perhaps for ever, she is not sure for how long. She realizes she is still quite drunk after all. She sits with her lips almost on his and traces the shape of his face with her fingertips.

'This has been the best night of my life,' she says softly. 'I feel – I feel like I just woke up.'

'Me also.'

They kiss again.

'But I think we should stop now,' he says. 'I am trying to be a gentleman, and remember what you said. And I don't want you thinking I am an axe murderer or sex maniac. Or . . . anything.'

Nell winds her fingers through his. 'Too late,' she says, and pulls him from the sofa.

Chapter Thirteen

Fabien wakes, and even before his eyes are fully open he knows something is different. Something has shifted, a weight no longer pressing down on him from the moment he sees light. He blinks, his mouth dry, and pushes himself up on his elbow. Nothing in the room is different, but he has a hangover. He tries to clear the fog in his head, and then he hears the sound of a shower.

And the previous night filters back to him.

He lies back on the pillow for a minute, letting the events come clear in his head. He remembers a girl dancing on a bar, a long walk through Paris, dawn spent in her arms. He remembers laughing, and a book of lists, and her sweet smile, her leg over his.

He pushes himself upright, pulls on his jeans and the nearest sweater. He walks to the coffee maker and refills it, then runs down the stairs to the bakery to grab a bag of croissants. As he returns, he opens the front door just as she comes out of the bathroom, wearing the green dress from last night, her hair wet around her shoulders. They stand still for a moment.

'Good morning.'

'Good morning.'

She seems to be watching him to see how he reacts. When he smiles, her smile is just as wide.

'I have to go back to the hotel and catch my train. It's . . . quite late.'

He checks his watch.

'It is. And I have to go to work. But you have time for coffee? I have croissants. You cannot leave Paris without coffee and croissants.'

'I have time if you have.'

They are a little awkward with each other now, the ease of last night fading. They climb back onto the bed, staying on top of the covers now, both dressed, close enough to be friendly but not enough to suggest anything else. She sips the coffee and closes her eyes.

'That's good,' she says.

'I think everything tastes good this morning,' he says, and they exchange a look. He eats swiftly, more hungry than he has felt for ages, until he sees he has eaten more than his share, and slows, offering her a croissant, which she waves away. Outside church bells are chiming and a small dog yaps.

'I have been thinking,' he says, still chewing. 'I have an idea for a new story. It is about a girl who makes lists for everything.'

'Oh, I wouldn't write that,' she says, giving him a sideways look. 'Who would believe it?'

'It's a good story. She's an amazing character. But she is a little too worried. She has to weigh up everything. The . . .'

'Pros and cons. For and against.'

'Pros and cons. I like this phrase.'

'And what happens to her?'

'I don't know yet. Something knocks her out of her habits.'

'*Bouf!*' she exclaims.

He grins, licks crumbs from his fingers. 'Yes. *Bouf!*'

'You'll have to make her very beautiful.'

'I don't need to make her beautiful. She is beautiful.'

'And very sexy.'

'You only have to see her dance on a bar to know it.'

He reaches across and feeds her a piece of croissant and, after a moment, they kiss. And then they kiss some more. And suddenly the croissants, the work and the train are forgotten.

*

Some time later Fabien pulls up in front of the hotel behind the Rue de Rivoli. The roads are quiet because it is Sunday. A few tourists stroll by, looking up to take pictures of the buildings. He is late for work, but the restaurant will have only a few customers now, regulars who come to sit with a dog and a newspaper, or tourists killing time until they are due to go home. But it will fill later, and by four o'clock it will be packed.

Behind him, he feels Nell release her arms from around his waist. She climbs off the seat and stands beside the bike. She pulls off the helmet and hands it to him. She peels his jacket from her shoulders and gives it back to him, so that she is standing there in her crumpled green dress.

She looks tired and untidy, and he wants to put his arms around her. 'Will you be warm enough, without a coat?' he says.

She tilts her head to one side. 'Funnily enough, I'm not feeling the cold today.'

'You sure you don't want me to take you to the station? You will be OK getting there? You remember what I told you about the Métro station?'

'You're already late for work. I'll find it.'

They gaze at each other. She shifts her weight from one foot to the other, her handbag dangling in front of her. Fabien finds he no longer knows what he wants to say. He takes off his helmet and rubs at his hair.

'Well,' she says.

He waits.

'I'd better get my suitcase. If it's still there.' She twists her hands around the handbag strap.

'You will be OK? With this Pete? You don't want me to go in with you?'

'Oh, I'm not worried about *him*.' She screws up her nose, as if he is of no importance. He wants to kiss it.

And he cannot help himself. 'So . . . Nell-from-England. Will I . . . see you again?'

'I don't know, Fabien-from-Paris. We don't really know anything about each other. We might have nothing in common. And we live in different countries.'

'This is true.'

'Plus we had one perfect night in Paris. It would be a shame to spoil it.'

'This is also true.'

'And you are a busy man. You have a job and a whole book to write. And you do have to write it, you know. Quite quickly. I'm anxious to hear what happens to this girl.'

Something has happened to her face, some subtle change. She looks relaxed, happy, confident. He wonders at what can change in twenty-four hours. He wishes he knew what to say to her. He kicks at the pavement, wondering how a man who prides himself on being good with words can find himself without a single one. She glances behind her at the hotel.

'This story of yours,' she says suddenly. 'I never asked. How does it end?'

His legs straddle the bike. He leans forward, his eyes not leaving hers, so that he is resting on the handlebars. 'I have no idea.'

She raises her eyebrows.

He says, 'I find that in the really interesting stories it is the characters themselves who decide.'

'Let's see what she decides, then.' She reaches into her bag and pulls out her notebook, handing it to him. 'Here. For your research. I don't think I need it any more.'

He looks at it. Her address and telephone number are written on the first page. He tucks it carefully inside his jacket. She leans forward and kisses him again, one hand on his cheek.

'So . . . we will see what happens,' he says, as she steps back.

'Yes. Yes, we will.'

They face each other on the empty pavement, and then, finally, when they can stand there no longer, he pulls on his helmet. With a roar of his engine and a wave of his hand, he rides off towards Rue de Rivoli.

Chapter Fourteen

Nell is still smiling as she walks into the hotel. The receptionist is still behind her shiny desk. She wonders if the woman has a home or just sleeps there, on her feet, behind the desk, like giraffes do. She realizes she should be embarrassed, turning up in last night's dress without her coat, but she cannot do anything but smile.

'Good morning, Mademoiselle.'

'Good morning.'

'I trust you had a good evening?'

'Lovely,' she says. 'Thank you. Paris is . . . so much more fun than I could ever have imagined.'

The woman nods to herself, and gives Nell a small grin. 'I am very happy to hear that.'

Nell takes a deep breath and looks over to the stairs. This is the bit she is dreading. For all her brave words to Fabien, she is not looking forward to Pete's accusations, or to his fury. She has wondered, privately, whether he will have done something horrible to her suitcase. He didn't seem like the kind of man to do such a thing, but you never knew. She stands there, bracing herself to go up to room forty-two.

'Can I help you with anything, Mademoiselle?'

She turns her head and smiles. 'Oh. No. I'm – I just have to go up and speak to my friend. He may . . . be a little cross that I did not include him in last night's plans.'

'I am sorry to tell you he is not here.'

'No?'

'A rule of the hotel. I realized after you left that we cannot have someone using the room who is not the person who booked it. And the room was in your name. So Louis had to ask him to leave.'

'Louis?'

She nods towards the porter, a man who is the size of two back-to-back sofas standing upright. He is pushing a small trolley loaded with suitcases. As he hears his name, he gives a small salute.

'So my friend did not stay in my room?'

'No. We sent him to the youth hostel. I'm afraid he was not very happy.'

'Oh!' Nell's hand has clapped over her mouth. She is trying not to laugh.

'I apologize, Mademoiselle, if this causes you any problems. But he was not on the original

booking, and he did not arrive with you so . . .
once you were gone . . . It was a matter of
security.' Nell notices the receptionist's mouth
is also twitching. 'A rule of the hotel.'

'A rule of the hotel. Quite. It's very important
to stick to hotel rules,' says Nell. 'Well. Um.
Thank you very much.'

'Your key.' The receptionist hands it to her.

'Thank you.'

'I hope you enjoyed your stay with us.'

'Oh, I did.' Nell stands in front of her and
has to fight the urge to hug the woman. 'Thank
you so much. Your hotel could not have
been . . . nicer.'

'That is very good to hear, Madame,' says the
receptionist, and finally, she turns back to her
papers.

Nell is walking up the stairs slowly. She has
just turned on her phone and the messages are
pinging through, one by one, the later ones
with lots of capital letters and exclamation
marks. Most she barely reads before she deletes
them. There is no point in spoiling her good
mood.

But the last one arrived at ten a.m. that
morning, from Magda.

Are you okay? We are all desperate for news. Pete sent Trish a really weird text last night and we can't work out what's going on.

Nell pauses outside room forty-two, her key in her hand, listening to the bells pealing across Paris and the sound of French people talking in the reception area below. She breathes in the smell of polish and coffee and the scent of her own grubby Saturday-night clothes. She stands for a moment, and remembers, and a smile breaks over her face. She types a text:

I had the best weekend away EVER.

Amy's Diary	Maureen Lee
Beyond the Bounty	Tony Parsons
Bloody Valentine	James Patterson
Blackout	Emily Barr
Chickenfeed	Minette Walters
Cleanskin	Val McDermid
The Cleverness of Ladies	Alexander McCall Smith
Clouded Vision	Linwood Barclay
A Cool Head	Ian Rankin
A Cruel Fate	Lindsey Davis
The Dare	John Boyne
Dead Man Talking	Roddy Doyle
Doctor Who: Code of the Krillitanes	Justin Richards
Doctor Who: Magic of the Angels	Jacqueline Rayner
Doctor Who: Revenge of the Judoon	Terrance Dicks
Doctor Who: The Silurian Gift	Mike Tucker
Doctor Who: The Sontaran Games	Jacqueline Rayner
A Dreadful Murder	Minette Walters
A Dream Come True	Maureen Lee
The Escape	Lynda La Plante
Follow Me	Sheila O'Flanagan
Four Warned	Jeffrey Archer
Full House	Maeve Binchy
Get the Life You Really Want	James Caan
The Grey Man	Andy McNab
Hello Mum	Bernardine Evaristo

Discover the pleasure of reading with Galaxy®

Curled up on the sofa,
Sunday morning in pyjamas,
just before bed,
in the bath or
on the way to work?

Wherever, whenever,
you can escape
with a good book!

So go on...
indulge yourself with
a good read and the
smooth taste of
Galaxy® chocolate.

Proudly supports

Read more at ⓕ Galaxy Chocolate

Quick Reads are brilliant short new books written by bestselling writers to help people discover the joys of reading for pleasure.

Find out more at **www.quickreads.org.uk**

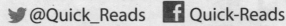 @Quick_Reads   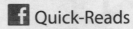 Quick-Reads

We would like to thank all our funders:

LOTTERY FUNDED

We would also like to thank all our partners in the Quick Reads project for their help and support: NIACE, unionlearn, National Book Tokens, The Reading Agency, National Literacy Trust, Welsh Books Council, The Big Plus Scotland, DELNI, NALA

At Quick Reads, World Book Day and World Book Night we want to encourage everyone in the UK and Ireland to read more and discover the joy of books.

World Book Day is on 5 March 2015
Find out more at **www.worldbookday.com**

World Book Night is on 23 April 2015
Find out more at **www.worldbooknight.org**

Red for Revenge

Fanny Blake

Two women, one man: code red for revenge...

Maggie is married with two grown-up children.
Her twenty-five year-old marriage
to Phil has lost its sparkle.

Carla is widowed. She understands life is short
so she lives it to the full. But is her new romance
all that it seems?

When the two women meet in the beauty salon,
they soon find they have more in common
than the colour of their nails.

The discovery that they are sharing the same
man is shocking. How will Phil be taught
a lesson or two he won't forget?

Orion

Start a new chapter

Pictures Or It Didn't Happen

Sophie Hannah

Would you trust a complete stranger?

After Chloe and her daughter Freya are rescued
from disaster by a man who seems too good to be
true, Chloe decides she must find him to thank him.
But instead of meeting her knight in shining armour,
she comes across a woman called Nadine Caspian
who warns her to stay well away from him. The man
is dangerous, Nadine claims, and a compulsive liar.

Chloe knows that the sensible choice would be
to walk away, but she is too curious. What could
Nadine have meant? And can Chloe find out the truth
without putting herself and her daughter in danger?

Hodder & Stoughton

Why not start a reading group?

If you have enjoyed this book, why not share your next Quick Read with friends, colleagues, or neighbours.

A reading group is a great way to get the most out of a book and is easy to arrange. All you need is a group of people, a place to meet and a date and time that works for everyone.

Use the first meeting to decide which book to read first and how the group will operate. Conversation doesn't have to stick rigidly to the book. Here are some suggested themes for discussions:

- How important was the plot?

- What messages are in the book?

- Discuss the characters – were they believable and could you relate to them?

- How important was the setting to the story?

- Are the themes timeless?

- Personal reactions – what did you like or not like about the book?

There is a free toolkit with lots of ideas to help you run a Quick Reads reading group at **www.quickreads.org.uk**

Share your experiences of your group on Twitter @Quick_Reads

For more ideas, offers and groups to join visit Reading Groups for Everyone at **www.readingagency.org.uk/readinggroups**

Other resources

Enjoy this book?

Find out about all the others at **www.quickreads.org.uk**

For Quick Reads audio clips as well as videos
and ideas to help you enjoy reading visit the
BBC's Skillswise website **www.bbc.co.uk/quickreads**

Skillswise

Join the Reading Agency's Six Book Challenge at
www.readingagency.org.uk/sixbookchallenge

THE READING AGENCY

Find more books for new readers at
www.newisland.ie
www.barringtonstoke.co.uk

Free courses to develop your skills are available in your
local area. To find out more phone 0800 100 900.

For more information on developing your skills
in Scotland visit **www.thebigplus.com**

Want to read more? Join your local library. You can borrow
books for free and take part in inspiring reading activities.